Library of Congress Cataloging-in-Publication Data   Gretz, Susanna.   Rabbit rambles on / Susanna Gretz. — 1st American ed.
p.   cm.   Summary: Duck and Frog decide to teach boastful Rabbit a lesson.   ISBN 0-02-737325-8   [1. Honesty—Fiction. 2. Animals—Fiction. 3. Friendship—Fiction.]   I. Title.   PZ7.G8636Rab   1992   [E]—dc20   91-17069

Rabbit Rambles On

Susanna Gretz

Four Winds Press   New York

Maxwell Macmillan International
New York   Oxford   Singapore   Sydney

Rabbit is boasting.

"I know how to do lots of tricks," he says.

"Like what?" asks Duck.
"What tricks?" asks Frog.

"Like . . . make chocolate sandwiches," says Rabbit.
"That's not a trick," says Duck.
"Anyone can do that," says Frog.

"Well, I also know how to balance things," says Rabbit.
"I can balance all my sandwiches on my nose."
"Go on, then," says Duck.

"I can't do it now," explains Rabbit,
"because I've eaten all my sandwiches."
"Hmm," says Frog.

"Anyway," says Rabbit, "I also know how to juggle."
"Do it, then," says Duck.

"I can't do it now," explains Rabbit,
"because I haven't got my juggling balls with me."
"Hmm, hmm," says Frog.
But Rabbit keeps rambling on.

"I can also throw a sandwich really high up," he says,
"and I can eat another one before it comes down!"
"I'll bet," says Duck.
"Do it, then," says Frog.

"Well," explains Rabbit, "I can't do it *now*–"
"Because you ate all your sandwiches," says Duck.
"That's right," says Rabbit, "*and* I've hurt my paw."

"I don't believe you," says Duck.

"That's nonsense," says Frog. "Let's all go on the seesaw."

"Okay," says Rabbit.

But Rabbit is heavier than Frog and Duck . . .

. . . so they soar high up in the air.
"I don't like this," says Frog. "I'm scared."

Then Duck has an idea.

"Let us down for a minute," she tells Rabbit. "It's a surprise."

Rabbit loves surprises. "Okay," he says.

He lets them down and hides his eyes.

"Almost ready," says Frog.
"Is it a nice surprise?" asks Rabbit.

"No peeking," says Duck.

"Surprise!" says Frog.
But now Rabbit is scared.
"Let me *down*!" he shouts.
"No!" yells Duck.

"Please!" calls Rabbit.
"It we let you down, will you stop making things up?"
asks Frog.

"I didn't make *everything* up," says Rabbit.
"What didn't you make up?"
"Well, I didn't make up the chocolate sandwiches,"
says Rabbit.

"You're sure?" asks Frog. She's feeling hungry.
Duck feels hungry, too.
"If we let you down, will you promise not to make things up?"
Rabbit promises.

"We could go to your house, Rabbit," says Duck.

"And you could show us how to make chocolate sandwiches,"
says Frog.

So they did.